THOMAS BREAKS
THE RULES

Random House

There is a line to a quarry at the end of Thomas's branch line. It goes for some distance along by the road.

Thomas was always very careful there in case anyone was coming.

"Peep, pip, peep!" he whistled, then people got out of the way and he puffed slowly along, with his cars rumbling behind him.

Early one morning there was a policeman standing close to the line. Thomas liked policemen. He had been a great friend of the officer who used to live in the village.

"Peep, peep! Good morning!" Thomas whistled.

Thomas expected that this new policeman would be as friendly as the other one. He was sorry to see that the policeman didn't look friendly at all.

The policeman was red in the face and very cross. "Disgraceful!" he spluttered. "I didn't sleep a wink last night–it was *so* quiet."

The policeman looked at Thomas. "And now," he said, "engines come whistling suddenly behind me!"

"I'm sorry, sir," said Thomas. "I only said 'good morning' to you."

"Where is your cowcatcher?" the policeman asked, sharply.

"But I don't catch cows, sir," said Thomas.

"Don't be funny!" snapped the policeman. He looked at Thomas's wheels. "No side plates, either!" he muttered, and he wrote in his notebook.

Then he spoke sternly to Thomas. "Engines going on public roads must have their wheels covered and a cowcatcher in front. You haven't so *you* are dangerous to the public."

"Rubbish!" said Thomas's driver. "We've been along here hundreds of times, and there has never been an accident."

"That makes it worse," said the policeman. And he wrote "REGULAR LAW-BREAKER" in his book.

Thomas's driver climbed back into the cab, and Thomas puffed sadly away.

Sir Topham Hatt was having breakfast. He was eating toast and marmalade. His wife had just given him some more coffee.

The butler came in.

"Excuse me, sir," he said. "You are wanted on the telephone."

"Bother that telephone!" said Sir Topham Hatt.

"I am sorry, my dear," he said a few minutes later. "Thomas is in trouble with the police, and I must go at once." He gulped down his coffee and hurried from the room.

At the station, Thomas's driver told Sir
Topham Hatt what had happened.

"Dangerous to the public, indeed! We'll
see about that!" said Sir Topham Hatt.

The policeman came onto the platform,
and Sir Topham spoke to him at once.
But however much Sir Topham argued
with him...

...it was no good.

"The law is the law," said the policeman
"and we can't change it."

Sir Topham Hatt felt quite exhausted.

"I'm sorry," he said to Thomas's driver.
"It's no use arguing with policemen. We
will have to make those cowcatcher things
for Thomas, I suppose."

"Everyone will laugh, sir," said Thomas,
sadly. "They will say that I look like a tram."
   Sir Topham Hatt stared at Thomas, and
then he laughed. "Well done, Thomas! Why
didn't I think of it before?" he said.

"We want a tram engine," he went on.
"When I was on my vacation, I met a nice
little engine called Toby. He hasn't enough
work to do, and he needs a change. I'll write
to his superintendent at once!"

A few days later Toby arrived.

"That's a good engine," said Sir Topham
Hatt. "I see that you have brought your
coach Henrietta with you."

"You don't mind, do you, sir?" asked
Toby, anxiously. "The stationmaster
wanted to use her as a henhouse, and that
would never do."

"No, indeed," said Sir Topham Hatt,
gravely. "We couldn't allow that!"

Toby made the freight cars behave even better than Thomas did.

At first, Thomas was jealous, but he was so pleased when Toby rang his bell and made the policeman jump that they have been firm friends ever since.

THOMAS

EDWAR

GORDON

HENRY

JAMES

PERCY

Based on *The Railway Series* by the Rev. W. Awdry

Photographs by David Mitton, Kenny McArthur, and Terry Permane
for Britt Allcroft's production of *Thomas the Tank Engine and Friends*

First American Edition, 1991.
Copyright © by William Heinemann Ltd. 1990. Photographs copyright © Britt
Allcroft (Thomas) Ltd. 1985, 1986. All rights reserved under International and
Pan-American Copyright Conventions. Published in the United States by
Random House, Inc., New York. Originally published in Great Britain as *Thomas
in Trouble* by Buzz Books, an imprint of the Octopus Publishing Group, London.
All publishing rights: William Heinemann Ltd., London. All television and
merchandising rights licensed by William Heinemann Ltd. to Britt Allcroft
(Thomas) Ltd. exclusively, worldwide.

Library of Congress Cataloging-in-Publication Data
Thomas in trouble.
Thomas breaks the rules / [photographs by David Mitton, Kenny McArthur, and
Terry Permane for Britt Allcroft's production of Thomas the tank engine and
friends].–1st American ed.   p.   cm.   Originally published: Thomas in
trouble. London :   Octopus Pub. Group, © 1990. "Based on the Railway series
by the Rev. W. Awdry"–T.p. verso.   SUMMARY: When Thomas the Tank Engine
gets in trouble with the police, Toby the Tram Engine comes to his aid.
ISBN 0-679-82088-4   [1. Railroads–Trains–Fiction.]   I. Mitton, David, ill.
II. McArthur, Kenny, ill.   III. Permane, Terry, ill.   IV. Awdry, W. Railway series.
V. Thomas the tank engine and friends.   VI. Title.   PZ7. T36947   1991
[E]–dc20   91-2428

Manufactured in Great Britain   10 9 8 7 6 5 4 3 2 1